The White Line

The
White
Line

poems by

Daniel David Moses

Fifth House Publishers
Saskatoon
Saskatchewan

Copyright © 1990 Daniel David Moses.

All rights reserved. No part of this book may be reproduced in any form or by any means, electronic or mechanical, without permission in writing from the publisher, except by a reviewer, who may quote brief passages in a review to print in a magazine or newspaper or broadcast on radio or television.

Thanks to the following magazines, journals, and anthologies where many of these poems appeared: *The Antigonish Review, Canadian Literature, CVII, Dandelion, event, The Fiddlehead, First Person Plural, Grain, Harper's Anthology of 20th Century Native American Poetry, The Magazine to Re-Establish the Trickster, Northward Journal, Poetry Canada Review, Poetry Toronto, Prism International, Quarry, Scree*(USA), *The Tamarack Review, This Magazine, Toronto Life, Waves,* and *Whetstone.* Thanks also to the Ontario Arts Council.

Canadian Cataloguing in Publication Data
Moses, Daniel David, 1952-
The white line
Poems.
ISBN 0-920079-68-7
I. Title.
PS8576.0747W45 1990   C811'.54   C90-097143-6
PR9199.3.M684W45 1990

Edited by Judith Fitzgerald.
Design: Robert MacDonald, MediaClones Inc.
Toronto Ontario, Banff Alberta, and Saskatoon Saskatchewan.

This book has been published with the assistance of
The Saskatchewan Arts Board and The Canada Council.

Fifth House Publishers

20 - 36th Street East
Saskatoon, Saskatchewan
S7K 5S8

Printed in Canada

For Blanche and David Moses,
my parents

The Fall

Song of the Worms

I welcome worms who swim up through the mud
by suggesting they come in from the rain.
I'm just another one of the Drowning,
and much friendlier than I've ever been.

I admit that my arms have gone loggy
but I embrace with my hair and my chill.
And these lips aren't prunes yet — they're still good for
a kiss — or the promise of survival.

Yes, if only they'd tell me the secret —
slip in this ear how to breathe underground —
I know we could share our futures and hopes,
could be sure not one of their squirm would drown.

But they don't seem to care about friendship,
they won't barter for so worldly a thing.
They know they're the throats who laud all matter;
I'm simply a church for their boring hymns.

You would think a prayer would mollify them,
but their long faces grow even more long.
As they swallow into the brain, it seems
a guttural kissing more than a song.

And that makes you believe they're excited
and glad — As if they could have our passion!
They're not much more than fingers stretching out
along the walls of their gloomy new home.

They don't mind that a skull isn't roomy.
Against the wetness that never will end,
they know they have to make some sort of stand.
They start a whirring I can't comprehend.

So I picture a spinning umbrella
making a similarly pleasant sound.
I guess I'm ready to bend my head in
on itself, away from the flooded ground.

Dandelions at Dusk

Struck by the tilting light,
the dandelions flare,
a fire in a match-
stick forest. So stop. Watch

it burn. Even that tame
a patch of flame teaches
something. Maybe that night
won't quite put the embers

out. Or maybe you learn
to forget. The field
flares up in stars. Daylight.
Do you remember it?

Poppies in November

    The scarlet springtime blooming on lapels?
    Mother must have planted such flat kisses.

    They're not bouquets. Frugal signals, shining
    that solitarily, the very stopped

    and formal hearts for this failing day.
    Yet how rawly the little blots open

    up! They mouth a cry perpetually.
    Oh, when will they be nothing more than cloth?

The Handkerchief

    Oh Nose, you're so sick.
    That worm of green phlegm
    has grown strong, so thick
    it breaks off the stem

    of breath. That flower —
    so white on your bed —
    nobody wonders
    what spotted it red.

The Fall

Apples glow
deliciousness across the long furrow

puddles where last night's
rain rivulets or sits

and clears, accepting the old
afternoon light. The mud halfway there holds

on so to the black rubber
boots that the picture

book falls open
faced and even in

a sock the child's foot is
naked to the splash. His cries

stream out like wordless
questions and the crow who passes

quickly through the open
seems to mimick them.

Florida Vacation

No, I won't post these cards. I'd rather keep
the swimsuit whites and cheap hybrid blues of
waterfall pools here in my hotel room.

I prefer to hoard my newly gathered
memories; only when I reach home will
I display them for family and friends.

Now, I can't imagine how I'll explain
my meals of mint ice cream or the daily
turning of my mind towards the smiling sun.

Perhaps I'm in love. The other men here
seem to be. The mossy beards a few of
them had have withered away. They're budding

again, those men in rows on the sand. Tans
ripen their skins more taut and thin and bright
— some lately discovered tropical fruit.

I'd join them there — but I fear they're bunching
odder colours up inside, tendrils that
will shoot out soon and strangle the unpruned palms.

The Sunbather's Fear of the Moon

Now that I'm out walking alone, old Bone
face looks jealous of the blood ruddiness
of my skin. Just let her try to scrape it
away and she will see it takes more than
petty metal to get to me, she'll see

how useless a good cool staring-down is
against skin this tough and crusty. And she
should identify with that. What the pale
fool won't understand quite as easily
is that my shine's not a reflected light

because it's always noon inside my chest
where day has a home the size of a fist.
I'm flushed with the heat of its love and of
the pleasures it brings through its bright
probing fingers and tongues. It's made me so

young I can go it alone. I don't need
that shine she gives to the land so wanly
old Boneface must know it can't cut the dark,
can't make it bleed anymore than I did
by day. The bit of bright blood I shed soaked,

as her light does, into the mud. Might be
red rain subterraneously. Or stars
for the troglodytes to see. It doesn't
matter. I refuse to shatter and set.
Let Boneface put on her idiot gape.

A Temperature at Dusk

The mosquitoes
cloud, their airy
storm shivers clean
across the flat
face of the pond.

It blows on mine
but I do not
respond, too caught
up in the way
the sky's ruddy

hues drain slowly
out and into
the west, into
the blue. Oh, too
at rest even

to wave away
the few testing
my flesh, needling
into the blue
inside my veins.

A bat-high squeak
flat in my ears
breaks through the calm
I'm in. I drain
out of my flesh

into the red
scene in the thin
brains in the pin
heads of hunters
falling through dark

at right angles
to everything.
Are we a rain
of claws and wings?
We are. We sing

about lightning
eyes and the glow
they get from meat.
A blood fever
swarms. We'll never

be calm again.
Nor will any
one. Writhing up
this din of grey
static hiss, trees

fall in love, grow
delirious
too. Why, the whole
world's giddily
malarial!

Under the bruised
sky, even you
who hate the night
go straight ahead
and wave goodbye.

A Seance

We've gathered our bodies like thunderheads
around this Ouija board. Look how it's laid
out — a prairie where our God has arrayed
His weird and skeletal herd. When our heads
nod careless as heaven and our fingers
weigh as little as rain, there in the board's
clear centre, this pointer shaped like our Lord's
dear Heart will dart about, heading letters
out. They'll take flight, flocking behind our eyes,
the words of His answer again spelled out
for taking stock, the promises held out
entire as rainbows. But first He tries
our faith. We wait for lightning in silence.
For frightening words, for thunderous sense.

Twinkle

There's no light around
the old place tonight

— just lawn so profound
you feel for each step.

And the old house too
looks a perfect hole,

standing over you
like space with no stars.

Is this the place where
you grew up? This dark

so far from the road
everything's quiet

— no wind, not even
in the Big Tree's top.

You can't watch your step.
So stop. Look up. Hold

your breath. You see? There
in between the beats

of your heart — is that
a toad that hops or

dew that you hear drop?
What else could it be?

Why is Polaris
shivering that way?

Starry Night

The Night has no lids on its eyes.
It stares even as it slumbers.
So we who've stayed in the city

this long get caught by a look. Few
of us take it for a come-on.
As usual we're unwelcome.

Some of us even see anger
in the way the lights waver. No
wonder most of us turn away.

We few who don't, who dare to meet
the stare, soon find it pays no
attention to us. In its view

we do not exist. We surmise
a blinding dream must be streaming
past inside those eyes. Why else would

they display such rapid movement?
Some few of us do try to stare
into the stare, to find out what

a dream that vast and bright could mean.
But one of us doesn't dare. I've had
nightmares before and need to know

first one thing for sure: How the Night
wakes up with its eyes already
wide open. Imagine always

dreaming the same. Would it start to
appal? What if we're mistaken?
Maybe it's not slumber at all.

The Old Guy

He saw a sun with
red eyes and claws, teeth
and a prickly coat.

He watched it come
scurrying over
glass broken as water

and easily slip
past the rusty barbs
of thick coiling wires.

He felt it brush
the wisps of his hair
with dusty straw colours

and didn't care
that his pate showed through —
a dented gilded globe.

He felt like just
another penny
lost in our dry cellar

and thought the sun
some god who gnawed and
breathed the word *tomorrow*.

The Politician's Miracle Play

The candidate claims to be God
but I warn you, he'll make this odd
demand: Outside the nunnery
gate he'll stay, bellowing, "Give me

a woman!" Should you try to put
him off, say, push a dead nun out
in a box, he'll have you believe
his passionate kiss can revive

her (and he might even suggest
that they'll become lovers who blast
off, a miraculous rocket
over the fields). You can bet

he won't admit an explosion
would happen or that ashes then
would fall like flies, blighting the grain
and your skin. You see how insane

it would be with my opponent
in power? Your flesh would be rent
by the rawest of flowers and
the taxes would use up the land.

Grandfather in Garden

*The soil's like small gravel
against my trowel. Is last night's
frost still in it? Have we seen
the last Indian-summer
day? Or will this go away
again this afternoon? How
hard it is on the knees. I*

*look up and see only thorns
and can't recall what colour
these roses were. I wonder
if I go find the shovel
will I be able to dig
potatoes? They ought to go
down the cellar. Just the thought*

*and I'm short of breath. I'll go
down to the orchard instead.
The apples are falling on
their own. Polished so they shine
like glass, Ma can put ribbons
on their stems and we'll give them
to all the kids at Christmas.*

Complaint of the Strawberry Fieldhand

It's taken me too long to learn that ripe
means just a terminal case of sunburn.

I'm halfway there already with my hands
medium rare and a temperature.

But strawberry flesh was so distracting —
a blush just showing through the patch's green.

It got me going so along the rows
I didn't care if anything went wrong.

I didn't know the berries in the shade
were hiding there — afraid of too much sun.

The colour wasn't other than sanguine
— though now it is. Now it's inside my skin.

Now that I've been over-exposed I can
see the reason for leaf cover and clothes.

I can see past the blush and down below
to berries the sun got at before me.

And their condition's not very pretty —
so far gone, there's no prognosis really.

How far beyond ruddy will these hands have
to go before they also lose their grip?

How much time have they got to turn the blush
into some sort of expression of love?

A jar, say, to carry into winter
and offer as a reminder of June.

How much sooner should they have started so
sun wouldn't burn now or they could wear gloves?

Or so the berry my chest hides wouldn't
beat now like it too is losing its grip.

Passing Above the Black River

The bridge glows the colour of bone
under its own hundred lights. Now
between those rows of blank glaring
faces, a car drives on. It holds

five who are full bellies. Their gloves
smear clearnesses on the windows
and wave away the dark that shows
through. Their words are about love and

have nothing to do with this cold
night that might be space. But the bridge
goes on so far the words die out
and the five are left at a brink.

At least one of them thinks even
the air between them is too rare.
Then the far bank comes alive with
a building of stars, a lantern.

Ballad from a Burned-Out House

Fire always wanted to marry Stone.
She claimed he alone could anchor her.
She travelled through the wood with her hair
loose and lifting almost to the sky.

Stone never dreamed he'd meet such beauty.
The heat of her kisses startled him.
Though he wished to be diamond and quartz,
his body quickly thickened and broke.

Fire shrouded herself in smoke and rain;
Stone covered his dark wounds with new grass.
Of course, they had no children or pain.
Theirs was a cool and perfect divorce.

In a Northern Car

With the old sun rolling over again
like the combustion of some oily ball
bearing — and a rash of lakes opening

up for spring with an iodine colour
staining their sheets at the edges — and dead
pine spikes crowning and stitching the granite

heights to the sky, yes, the world passing by
seems an alien one, a world too sick
and sluggish to accept. And with the few

birches and many elms rubbing their chalks
and charcoals and a leafless gloom into
the windows of the train while closing in

on the line — and the land's undulations
wearing slow and rough spots even into
the straights of the shivering tracks — this ride

is a trying ride, too private and dull
to attend. With the coach being carried
and rocked like a bauble by a roadbed

unfit for its ties, infected with frost,
with passengers like lushes stumbling or
lying around, their eyes vague and dying

like the ends of cigarettes and their tongues
failing the names on depot signs — the head
becomes this restless chamber travelling

soundless as a suitcase, full of a hushed
rhythm pressing the air, a gravel voice
insisting *This is. This is.* But who cares?

Ascension in June

Ascension in June

It's good to get above it,
all the pollen weather, up
where the thunderheads bulge, grand
as thrones. From here you can't see
their bottoms, dark as the mouths

of bells. From here they're bound east,
calm as a fleet of boredoms.
Here you forget how you broke
out in sweat like a glass, how
your hands wilted at the blue

perforated perfection
of your ticket. You even forget
the yoke of your luggage. And all
those kisses evaporate from your cheeks.
You mold to your chair and see

the perfumed ladies with
their permanent hair. They slide the trays
down the upholstered aisles
on words that go hush. How
to recall the summer's hot breath

when the drinks come served with lemon
slices and smiles? The steward
is mannequinly handsome
and the wind wears a white mask
and stares in through the portholes

trying to catch the movie,
so silently beautiful. With both
the wind's and these mutterings
muted by silver and steel,
I feel very much at home.

Of Course the Sky Does not Close

Of course, when you've been unhorsed
by thirst, you tend to lie where
you've landed. Who's got the strength
or breath or backbone to move
— or even think about it?

Of course, you believe your ears
and eyes — though their energy's
so low you shouldn't. They seem
to tell you the sky's open
only for your benefit!

Of course, that may be the truth
for all they can know. With air
this dry, each sound turns vague and
dusty and all the light so
coarse, it callouses your sight.

Of course, you'll mistake your horse
(if it trots back) for a cloud,
say, with thunder cracks. You took
these oats dangling in your eyes
for birds too distant to hear.

Of course, you take your own breath
and the grit of dust for wind
and the taste of cumulus;
you're expecting there to be
a storm closing up the sky.

Of course, the sun is the one
white staring eye in the wide
blue face of the sky, a face
so open you can deny it
nothing and offer your eyes.

Of course, the sky prefers ponds.
It gently plucks each one from
the face of the land. The sky
couldn't care less about you
— or if your eyes get plucked too.

Of course, now you're so angry
and jealous, you've energy
enough to realise how
mad you've been, how pitiful
your situation's become.

Of course, you worry the sky
is so stupid it won't see
when you're dead. Will it keep on
trying to stare you down, not
realising it has won?

Of course, you are mistaken.
The sky is full of remorse.
The darkness in its face cries
the eyes of the land back in,
will even water your horse.

Meteor

Coming from
the starry
dark it slips

into air and
incandescence
quick as

a drop of
mercury.
Down here to

marry
glory, it
flares and strobes

the city.
With its day-
coloured light

it blinds and
woos the mind
made of earth

where the sky
already
is buried.

Drowning Song

    I fall through
    the river
    the sun shrinks.

    My hands turn
    beautiful
    as ink. Fish

    like statues
    oh and kiss.
    Their eyes are

    air. My voice
    keeps bobbing
    in their mouths.

Bee Muse

Arthritic? A shrug. Now
that even her tongue cricks,
she rarely speaks. (Never
sings.) It's not that words hurt
all that much. The joints of
her fingers and wrists ache

worse than words ever will;
throb like wings whenever
she clutches anything.
And she still uses them.
No. What's got her almost
shut up is a simple

question of aesthetics.
When words fall flat out of
her mouth and buzz around
on their backs — even when
she tries by whispering
to lighten or disguise

the dark drone they've become —
it's easy to guess why
she usually acts dumb.
But what's with this crooking
forefinger? You lean in
closer to see just how

beautifully the skin
of her throat crinkles as
she confides by way of
excusing her silence:
*I guess I'm some sort of
waxwork*. That's why you're caught

by the laugh that comes next.
Like the back of a hand,
an ugly little swarm,
it helps you understand
how this old proud woman
would prefer to simply

move her hand or shoulder,
to believe that gesture
tells more than words now can.
She lifts her arm up round
the nape of your neck and
hugs you so tight her wax

dry lips touch your ear, so
close she is sure none of
her words will fall unheard
as she questions — almost
forgetting to whisper —
about what must seem to

her a most important
rumour: *Did you read it?*
That story in the news
paper? About a man
who got his hand stung. Bees
or mosquitoes, I can't

recall which. Anyway,
it cured his arthritis.
Can you imagine that?
The things they print these days!
And that clumsy laugh breaks
her confidence again.

She shrugs, shakes her head, then
goes on whispering, but
about balmier things,
while you're imagining
she must dream in her naps
of her hands reaching out

towards a bright swarm of bees;
of the arms of the swarm
returning her embrace;
of her tongue flying through
speech and song, of its neat
tip stung back into grace.

The Hands

Yes, our faces are ten blanks
but bearded with the ghosts of
quarter moons. So we are wise,
wiser than you who go clothed
in fur, than you who have eyes.

Crow Out Early

The only one who speaks to this long rain
is that crow sitting on a pole like old
Raven, spitting out caws in pairs. He got
out of dreams on this wrong side of the bay.

Over there a foghorn makes a four-note
effort Crow can't comprehend. It's not like
even the loudest moans of his friends who
keep asleep, their effort to ignore how

this pressing fall of clouds has made a pine
the only place to settle. This makes Crow
with folded wings a black and glistening
pair of hands and his cries, a quick prayer, reach

out through the fog. His eyes get a shimmer
and his ears a song, both like the run off
gurgling at road edge. He sees the stones there
washing strong bodies egg bright, beetle slick.

The Corn

I'd already lost my hair. Now my sun-
fed children have been taken somewhere. Next

I'll lose these comfortable shoes of mud
to the cold, will be unconcerned. I no

longer need a firm foothold after all.
There's no flood of light anymore — to stand

in, to turn towards. The low sun's a trickle
that lays only shadows out (and they don't

move or fulfill one or feed some). Nor do
they do a thing for one's colour. One's left

with just these growing crystals of frost. No
childish ears to get brightly wet behind,

no hands to hold as you stand whispering
about the land. No one you could even

wave hello or goodbye. My hands carressed
the emptiness, grew as heavy as ice.

They dropped off; and, soon I'd guess the rest of
me will be ready to follow. Down through

the ice-bound soil to underground fields where
stars are planted in hills. At least that's what

I've seen, staring through the frost. Light will not
be lost but will grow and bud green again.

Inukshuk

You were built from the stones,
they say, positioned
alone against the sky
here so they might take
you for something human

checking the migrations.
That's how you manage this,
standing upright despite
the blue wind that snow is,
this close to Polaris.

Still, the wind worries
you some. It's your niches
which ought to be empty.
Nothing but lichen grows
there usually. Now

they're home to dreams. Most come
from the south, a few from
further north — but what flows
out of their mouths comes from
no direction you know.

They keep singing about
the Great Blue Whale the world
is; how it swims through space
having nightmares about
hunters who only hunt

their brothers — each after
the other's snow-white face.
How beautiful frozen
flesh is! Like ivory,
like carved bone, like the light

of Polaris in hand.
So it goes on and on,
the hunting refrain. Dead
silence would be better,
the Pole Star overhead.

The wind agrees, at least
wants to stop up each niche.
How long can you stand it
— that song, the cold, the stones
that no longer hold you

up now that they hold you
down? Soon the migrations
recommence. How steady
are you? Dreams, so they say,
also sing on the wing.

The Persistence of Songs

The people feed from the river and conceive songs.
But the strangers with the dead heads march towards the long
edges of their own blades. They see a thundering
fog along the horned horizon and turn around
to stalk the rising sun. They find four lanterns made
of skin arrayed along the river, the people
still feasting within. The strangers feed off their own
anger, flooding the river with blood. The four songs,
who are the children, go dumb and their white dogs mad
before the people have the strangers rounded up.

They bind them with skin from the fog and throw them in;
then, they wait for the river to heal. They try
to feast again. They pray to the children. By noon
the river grows an old skin and the children fade.
In the cold mud the strangers congeal. A fog
bleeds from the river, drowns the lanterns and stops up
the ears of the people with a dull, three-note song.
The strangers are praising honed edges and the white
meat of their own bodies. They curse the sun and vow
the moon turns so perfectly round they will square it.

They lurch up through the river's dull skin and begin
the marching again. The people search in the skin
for reflected light, the sunset or a lantern,
then assume the skin as mourning. The procession
the people enter tracks the moon through fog, cuts it
into quarters. And black dogs track the procession.
They feed off their own hunger and conceive a song
in praise of a perfect horizon made of meat.
That song fades; but, the four songs, who are the children,
return with horned heads. They feed from ears and edges.

Rain Forest

    Down from the limbs that cloud the light
    the dry brown rain continues its dark

    traditional fall into earth;
    and, though the hunched backs of roots break it,

    stall it, it still gradually
    makes its way into the soil and

    the mushrooms that overnight lift
    up various caps make the dry and

    traditional sort of splash, one
    that lasts only long enough to catch

    the light off the regular rain
    flashing past, a wet sort of lightning

    that strikes the traditional hue
    of the sky deep into the soil.

Dandelion Salad Day

The dandelion
spots on the season's
coat? That's not a rash;
but, it is breaking
out fast in this heat.

What does it suggest?
Simply that toothy
greens have gorged upon
the sun in these last
forty-eight hours.

Quite the light diet.
It's got the season
out of kittenish
camouflage colours.
The fevers that force

sweat or freckles (or
worse) out of our skins
have coaxed that brassy
flowering, those small
roars of yellow. How

this one purrs under
your chin! It's this hue's
day we loll around
in, the air licking
at our hair, at grey

puffs. Where did those few
dandelion greens
ever find enough
moon today to gorge
on and get that way?

The Blindman's Bluff

A hand. Just a hand. Is that asking for so much?
A hand with a sample case that's almost nothing
tonight because sales went so well. A hand

and not a touch. You can keep your pity, your love.
I'm like you; above all that. Whatever I need
I get in the city, either credit or cash.

A hand clutching my own to make me feel welcome
is what I'm looking for. It isn't yours? Aren't you
my neighbour next door? Can't you remember my face

and ignore what holds you back? Behind this dark
pair of glasses, they're open, empty, bland. There's no
way you can be caught and held by them. Or even

be pulled in. They're no good for giving directions
or even for saying goodbye. One thing they might
not be bad at is the casting of looks askance.

Of course I'm neither beggar nor witch. I'm the man
next door, the man who's in business, who can and does
guarantee this condition can't be caught by touch.

Vision, on the other hand, is a contagion
that you catch like a cold. When you're off on your own
it takes a hold of you. The only thing to do

is see it through. Your eyes start running with the sights.
Who knows what you might see? Not me. I care too much
about my business. Everyday I want to hear

the way each coin or foot falls or the way the voice
breaks as each customer makes the choice. I always
know where I'm going. I recognize each street's noise.

I know I've somehow come round to the lake tonight.
I make out far down the sound of waves against rocks.
So, can you understand what they sell with such grand

sales talk? At this height this almost empty case
is a weight and my face to you I know must look
like the night's. Help me find the dark glasses I lost.

Crystal Beach

The sand (so many mirrors)
gathering up the sun
won't let it disappear

like our reflections have
into the funhouse mirrors,
like the rolling mirrors of

the dark waves do. That's what
drew us here, isn't it?
That's what drew me to you.

You were the glass my light
gathered in, shiny, new.
Your body held my own

sharply in focus; flesh
again after hours
running to fat and thin

and almost losing sight
of itself in the waves
of the mirrors in the house

of fun. I swam on waves
of your body, a fish
made of shadow often

in flight above a tide
made of skin. This began
when the roller coaster

waves threw us together
and ended in this flood
of sun and burning mirrors.

No wonder we now wear
others over our eyes,
ones dark and cool as waves,

trying to see beyond
the shifting of the bright
sand we've landed on. What

about light going down
a last time, settling at
the bottom of a mirror

tarnished and drowned? We see
only this land of tan,
of rolling dark bodies

and not how a hand, held
up against the sun, shows
shadows of bones. We do

not reflect upon that
sort of thing. There is no
need. Not here. For this is

the land of many mirrors
and every one of them
has done with shattering.

We'll never be stuck with
all their years of bad luck.
We're too quick for this sand.

We'll never disappear.
This is our stand. Even
night won't make our stars fall.

Downtown Temperature

The heat has exhausted
even itself. It lies
tonight on the city
streets, unable to fall
into the dark of sleep.

The glow in the air keeps
re-opening its eyes
and asphalt (of course) makes
uncomfortable sheets.
Oh, it tries to lie still.

Just the twitch of a toe
echoes so much; it sounds
like the underground flow
of the subways. No one
can rest through that. The low

and impenetrable
ceiling of haze presses
down on its empty chest.
It hears through the walls each
rise and fall of the hearts

asleep in small, sublet
apartments. It envies
that easy beat. The heat
rises and turns an eye
to each window. In each

room, where the fans only
go through the motions, lie
bodies that dream. It fears
it won't ever do that.
Then, the wings of a bat

turn arrhythmically
through its head and the heat
begins a waking dream.
Constellations, it seems
are about to rise up

from those beds. The heat shakes
that off and sees instead
bright sweat beading. It might
fall into sleep and dreams
could it clutch one such star.

My Last Seance

Tonight I thought the crystal might not
open. I thought the questions might be
a problem. I thought — I'm not sure what.

Our medium did her regular
routine — but tonight I got anxious.
Was something really interfering?

Madam White waved a hand from this plane
toward that — and had to do so again
before I cued back in to my part.

Then my blind Mister Black implored her
to try harder. His anxiety
tonight quickly convinced the others.

The ones beside him in the circle
held my hands even tighter. Someone
actually took over his plea.

I sighed — her cue to end the suspense —
so she tried even harder. The trance
she began I recognised at once.

The eyelids tight and quivering and
the loose voice muttering the words from
some intermediary spirit.

But tonight I could not hear it, not
after I'd seen how both her eyes and
the crystal suddenly unshuttered.

That shining was not the usual
one. The hidden spotlight was not on.
From what other site could white light come?

A man to my right said he thought I
ought to ask the first question. But none
came into my head. Instead that light

did. That light. And all the blind looks of
those kind waiting eyes. I realised
the questions I'd forgotten were lies.

I felt so small — the same size, say, as
my image in the crystal's surface —
I couldn't keep up the disguise tonight.

I took the dark glasses off, meaning
to confess. My opened eyes took in
the crystal: the crystal took me in.

I guess I went into a trance and
answered each question myself, passed on
the ususal banal messages.

But what I recall is passing through
the crystal's wall and finding myself
in the middle of the light inside.

I remember too — I can't forget —
the igniting of my hands. The bones
had opened up so many new suns.

I can't remember any thoughts. Still,
there wasn't any space in my head
once the crystal had replaced the skull.

While Madam White, smiling, excited,
did congratulate my Mister Black,
asking only for more warning next

time, I think I might try moving on.
I think carrying on, carrying
this, can't be done, unless I'm alone.

Your Parents' Hands

Your hands either dream or have memories
not their own. In one, they're hands belonging
to a woman who uses them to touch
a man; to lift him up like a column
of clay. In another, it's a man to
whom your hands belong. He's using them on

the woman, spinning her out like a cloud.
In one even more like a dream, all four
of those hands appear, each one of them off
on its own somewhere, trying to unfold
its fingers enough to get a hold on
a star. At least, that's what you remember.

And then there's this hut, mud and sticks, this man
asleep dreaming of your hands; the woman
by the door keeping one eye on the fire
and the other on the mist and the firs.
Then it's the woman who's sleeping under
the stars, dreaming your hands; the man who sits

with his back to the warm, his eyes scanning
the plain. And there's something else that must be
a dream: Hands pressing so tightly together
the crescent moons on their nails grow brighter,
grow so full, one pull tighter, in fact, makes
them all ignite and conflagrate. The flash

fire that sun is dries the sweat off your hands.
All each retains is a palmful of salt
that sparks as you pick it out of the dark
cold ashes. And in the last scene your hands
remember or dream; each palm of them holds
a different horizon. The first waves

goodbye to the moon while its opposite
opens up to welcome the sun. The third
at the top and the fourth at the bottom
of the world. Each holds onto one half of
a pair of hands so new, they've nothing to
remember. They dream. They dream about you.

A Shaman Song Predicting Winter

The sun is running down, so the White
Bear says, *circling and wearing the track
it cut into the sky right through. Soon*

*it will roll into the ocean. Though
it can't drown, that'll sure cool it off.
If you kayak out far enough and*

*look in, you'll see it looking up through
the night black waves, looking right at you
jealously, shivering like the moon.*

The White Line

Admonition to an Ice-Skating Child

When the mercury sun sinks below zero
pretend you're blind so you won't be afraid
you can't see. Listen for your mother and
don't tap too loudly. The river's lonely
under its white sky. With fish eyes frozen
it sees only bubbles of dark. It twists
around searching for a deep place it passed
too quickly to know. It's sure someone's there.
If the river hears you, its wings will lift
and flicker through its clouds saying, *Sh!*
Now you're not lost. Its tongues will unfold
and wash your face, will wrap your hands in muffs
of frost. You'll slide off its smile into black
kisses. You'll forget you need to grow old.

An Offering of Frost

Somnambulant and shoeless, the Moon still
manages to drop the hair she loses
like handkerchiefs along the garden path.

Nevertheless, the last leaves stop their dry
laughter and turn away while the stones act
only as mannerly as a clenched smile.

The Moon's emptiness cannot be ignored,
no matter how slightly it sways. It hangs
as ill and pale as a bed in a mirror.

Not one stone would stay unturned away — would
face that colour — could it do otherwise.
It's so morbid that they envy the leaves.

The Moon wobbles along, hiding that grin
and those eyes with a dark fan, showing off
ancient blemishes only to shed them.

Though they shred like bandages, it doesn't
hurt. Not a twitch. She's numb with a mummy's
happiness and she'll be like that for years.

The way she litters the path but preserves
her dignity — it is nothing less than
she deserves. It's perfect, the way she stares.

And that's why hushed leaves flee into their own
shadows, and why stones return the Moon's cold
shoulder, pretending the night's full of stars.

Grandmother in White

*No, I don't want to sit still in my sweater
but with all these sheets I feel snowed in.*

*Besides, where could I go tonight? The halls are
all closed. I'll leave the light off — the way*

*it glares when I already am blind enough.
My nurse on her rounds looks in, looking*

*so much like the moon that I know she's smiling
but otherwise I am quite alone*

*and quite at a loss. I keep dreaming
up flowers though I've got no crêpe or tissue*

*papers to make them come true and my fingers
feel bony, the skin worn through, useless*

*unless I can peel it back into
petals and become my own best handicraft.*

*Yes, my hands cupped together on the bedclothes
have already gone half numb and pale*

*as frost before dawn. Before long my nurse will
come by and see an Arctic blue rose.*

Grandmother of the Glacier

The icefield she had in her head started
sliding the instant she died. *Was murdered*
would be more precise — would also explain
how her corpse became this high and open

ravine. But who's got the wit to split words
when that ice is coming at us? The world
can't ever again be that room we sat
in a circle in — the mainland rain hard

on a window as we listened to her
trying to explain about words. *Winter,*
she grinned. *That's the constant thought behind all
our words. In Canada we never can*

forget the edge on the wind. But the edge
on a knife cut in, cutting off more than
her words. So now it's hard to remember
how that edge and this cold thought grinding down

out of her head ever seemed separate.
Now they're a mouth that bites off and chews and
it's getting so close that breath flakes like snow.
So we go mute too — that mouth edge so red

that words drop from our own lips like stones. None
is as finished as those of hers that fell
into our hands. But the stars now are shards
of ice — they too are cutting in. There's no

time for her method — to split and polish
words against our own skin. Is that how hers
got so coarse she could embrace and contain
not only the stars but the rest of this freeze?

Her body's been swallowed. Ours may be next.
But even though we throw them in, her words
keep surfacing. May ours too be heard from
again — edging some terminal moraine.

A Mansion in Winter

Among the beautiful
charcoal shards of the wall
the cold flowed so thickly

it shone. Where the door once was
I paused and fell through
boards that broke

into air that kept on
breaking out
in musk. The roof dipped

its sooty ribs and stepped
after me in
to the opened cellar where

stars came glinting
like ivory out
of the stones. I got

an itch crystallizing
in my throat and in the black
was alone, a hoary

elephant
waiting among
the pieces of the floor

for the moonfaced hunters
to return with their angers
to their trap full of tar.

The End of Night

Here in the black dream you're small once again
against the tall back of your grandfather's
rocking chair. And you're following a crack
between two boards of the veranda, towards

and over its brink. And there the lawn and
the garden are dark and still as a dried
spill of ink. And only along what should
be the dawn horizon is there any

illumination. There it comes, a grey
flicker showing through that line of thunder
clouds. And it comes quicker now, the closer
together those clouds get, the more lightning

they exchange. Now they let an electric
white rising sun erase the dark. The land's
too bright to read in the glare, paper no
longer marked by trees or fences. Your eyes

start burning and there's no turning away
from the solar wind. Your grandfather's chair
is carrying you into ashes. You're
in the white dream going blind once again.

Paper

    We are so well-mannered we never move
without sending a letter-of-intent
months in advance. Always we sign it *Love*
though we know little of hearts or rose scent.
We wouldn't recognize red if it fell
out of our mouths. Its very existence
depends on rumours and it's possible
to believe only so much that's nonsense.
It's too bad if anyone imagines
words have ever bled when the clean blackness
of letters on this paper should imply
that it's easy to live. You can't deny
the truth of salutation or addresss —
there is nothing but white between the lines.

Aren't You Tired of Fire?

Consider this flake
the wind's lost tooth
or the ghost of an eye.

Isn't it beautiful
turning its symmetries?
It's the spinning coin

you use to buy
eternity. Take it.
It won't ring

false. It's the
prize for you and nothing
to stagger away from

or shiver at.
It can't bite anymore
or stare. Lay it

down, a sheet on a bed.
See how breath spreads
out like a mirror?

Come and lie
down. Your father
is here, feeding

the dreams he once
owned. Come.
Your mother is here and she

eats up her own
face
out of the air.

The Letter

This favour you're asking of yourself
may not do you any good — but tell
yourself it will, tell yourself it should

save your skin, should put the fire out of
your flesh before it's too late, before
much more of this heat that alternates

with ash uses you up. There's hardly
enough left to feel embarrassed for
being so easy to read — hardly

enough left to make the request. Please,
that scrap of you says, Give the letter
up. Feed it to the fire. It's easy

for the fire to digest. Paper is
the brighter fuel of the two after
all. Flesh, with its blushes and veins, looks

so foolish beside it. It would seem
only just — the fair exchange. The fire
can take to the paper and leave you

alone. How good to know that reading
the letter would never again push
the fire inside to ignite. The hand

writing on it would simply become
black and white again, so easily
read that as you lean your head over

the flame and catch some word, some phrase for
the last time — perhaps your own, perhaps
that other name being blacked out and

flaked into smoke — your face in a light
coat of soot will begin to cool down
and be not only illegible

but after you've washed it clean, you'll see
the skin smooth out, become unlined, free
again, a new page turning over.

Snow is Not Paper

He writes that he tried to murder Winter.
He could take no more of its cruelty.
He thought dismemberment ought to do it,
so he started flake by flake. And flake by
flake by flake, the edges caught in and slit

through his skin. It surprised him that the breaks
ached like paper cuts, stabbed so much that not
till the cold bled in past his shivering
and had congealed, could he realise
his mistake. He should have tried fire. Even

now near the equator he hears the cold
crack and groan, grinding like a glacier
inside of him. Between the joking lines
he writes about indigestion I can
read the postscript he'll never add after

the *adios. Unless Winter,* it runs,
grows kindly and old — or dies — soon the frost
will break open my bones. Oh, the marrow
at least will be clear. Like a pardon — or
summer — or a memory made of snow.

The Pass

I saw the day fall away behind us
in the rear-view mirror — so I don't know what
you are looking forward to with your foot
to the floor. I was taking the mountains
in all afternoon. Now my attention's

gone as limited as my sight. I do
speculate a bit about rocks and snow
and frozen lakes — about how far below
us in the blackness they are. But mostly
I stare into the few seconds of white

centre line the headlights find. The higher
along the highway the pickup pushes
through the pass, the more that uncertain line
is the windshield for what's left of my mind.
This truck is — how high now? How far below

zero? Beyond radio and nearly
blind. The tires would be spinning in space
without this through line we are holding close.
That deer that just makes it across — the white
tail a glare — does not shake you. So this

uncertain constellation where the rock
wall falls away — either a reflection
or a town down under the glacier
lake — only makes me look forward now to
shaking into line the stars that remain.

Bearwalk

At night I stroll behind my eyes,
trying to avoid the bears.
Now they're invisible in the snow,

I've got to take care not to sweat,
not to let them know I know they're there,
what they are, dangerous.

If I'm ambushed I pretend
the bear's an igloo; walk up and push
my head into its maw

and comment on the reek.
Make a bear question the repute
of its jaws and it's spiritless.

Point at its mouth and say
A star! Is it Christmas?
and it's done with. I've tripped on

bones of bears who'd bitten
their own hearts out. Once they're extinct
I'll never wake up dead.

I Am Not a Snowshoe Rabbit

The goggles have bone lenses. They admit
only polarised light and the horizon.
I track the bright cloud which hoards all heat

till a cough breaks my attention. The raw note
shatters and sifts. I search the white shadows
for its source. The only tongues and throats

are hissing drifts. There are no other ghosts.
A hollow looms dark as a mouth which I greet
with lungs open wide for breath. For breath

is the one body, it is what the cold eats.
It climbs the hills, all ice and frozen air
and is even beautiful when it falls.

A Story from the Mouths on a Beach

In the season of floes in the midst of
the pack a single great fish appeared and
along with some dozens of bodies of
ice came into these shallows on the flux
of the flood and bobbing here in the wash
of the ebb was stranded and exposed to

the air. Now it sang a song as these fish
usually do about the hues of
oceans and skies — though the version this sang
sinking into itself sounded as poor
as the hiss of a wave as it dies. Still
that got the attention of a babble

of children and drew them down from the cliffs
into a discussion of the fish's
skin and the stars they thought were beginning
inside. *Soon this fish will be up so high —
a new constellation,* sighed one of them.
We ought to try for immortality,

came the suggestion and the rest agreed.
Now in their concentration, incising
their names into the fish's skin, not one
of them caught the last note escaping from
its flesh, ringing like one of those bubbles
that breaks through the surface of these shallows

on the calm evenings in the season
of flies. Had they heard, would any have been
interested? Only the unearthly
attracts them. Now the children hurried off
toward some other song — it sounded as rich
as a cough — and so they could not witness

the way the skin of the fish went cold,
the way it iced over like the nameless
upper parts of this river must the first
nights of the season of wind. None of them
saw the final closing, each eye sinking
into decomposing flesh, each a half-

accomplished wink, a denial of both
twinkling and watery horizons. Now
only we who amplify and echo
the flood and ebb of your blood, who were washed
free of our tongues by the air and exposed,
can testify that the single great fish

did not completely die. Inside the few
remaining parts of it the song about
the hues of oceans and skies is still ringing
sweetly. And friends, those ice-coloured parts
will sing the song out again — though not till
the end of the final season of whites.

The Line

This is not the poem, this line
I'm feeding you. And the thought
that this line is not the poem
is not it either. Instead
the thought of what this line is
not is the weight that sinks it
in. And though this image of
that thought as a weight is quite
a neat figure of speech, you
know what it's not — though it did
this time let the line smoothly
arc to this spot, and now lets
it reach down to one other,
one further rhyme — the music
of which almost does measure
up, the way it keeps the line
stirring through the dampening
air. Oh, you know you can hear
the lure in that. As you know
you've known from the start the self
referring this line's doing
was a hook — a sharp, twisted
bit of wit that made you look
and see how clear it is no
part of this line or its gear

could be the poem. Still it cast
and kept the line reeling out
till now at last the hook's on
to itself and about to
tie this line I'm feeding you
up with a knot. Referring
to itself has got the line
and us nowhere. So clever's
not what the poem is about
either. We're left hanging there
while something like a snout starts
nudging at your ear, nibbling
near my mouth — and it's likely
it's the poem about to take
the bait. From the inside ought
to be a great way to learn
what the poem is. And we'll use
this line when the poem's drawn it
taut and fine as breath to tell
what we know, where we are and
where we'll go — unless the line
breaks. How would it feel, knowing,
at last, what the poem really
is, to lack the line to speak?